# PuddleDuck

Story by Nancy Hundal
Pictures by Stephen Taylor

 HarperCollins*Publishers*Ltd

Produced by Caterpillar Press for
HarperCollins Publishers Ltd
Suite 2900, Hazelton Lanes
55 Avenue Road
Toronto, Canada M5R 3L2

96 97 98 99  First Edition  7 6 5 4 3 2 1

Canadian Cataloguing in Publication Data
Hundal, Nancy, 1957–
Puddleduck

Hardcover ISBN 0-00-224012-2
Paperback ISBN 0-00-648117-5
I. Taylor, Stephen, 1964 – . II. Title.

PS8565.U63P84 1994 jC813'.54 C94-930369-0
PZ7.H86Pu 1994

Bianca's story

*Nancy Hundal*


For my family

*Stephen Taylor*

That one spring, Bianca knew that Puddleduck would come back. He had been gone a long time — since the summer before. But when she saw from her window the gray sheets of rain slicing through the clouds, she knew her Puddleduck was coming too.

His lavender rain coat and navy boots had been
too warm on that summer's day. But when she asked,
he shook his beak no, duck sharp. His eyes were shiny
black, watching a pair of brown ducks glide and dip in the
pond by the picnic blanket. When her sister called her to
watch the butterflies dance in the raspberry thicket, Bianca
leapt up. Afterwards, she was glad she'd turned back and patted
the tangly tuft on the top of his head.

When she came back, Puddleduck was gone. The grown-ups
hadn't really been watching, of course, but they said no one had
come near the blanket. No children passed, no wild animals prowled.
Only the furious sun knew where a duck of fur and stuffing had gone.
Even the brown ducks had swum away, tucking the sad secret under
their feathers.

It took Bianca a long time to fall asleep that night. It was the first time she could ever remember sliding down the long tunnel into sleep without Puddleduck beside her. Her room seemed darker. Her bed seemed bigger. With no sleepy quacks whispered in her ear, the room was so quiet that it was loud.

Bianca asked her father to tell her the story of how she got Puddleduck. He told her once. He told her twice. The third time, she told him. Then she made up a song about it, and drew a picture about it. The picture showed a hospital nursery full of babies, each with a tiny bear or lamb or bunny in their crib. All the babies were crying except one, the smiley baby with a Puddleduck resting his beak on her leg. His glinty eyes made sure nothing would make *his* baby cry.

All that summer, Bianca searched for Puddleduck. She climbed the cherry tree in the back yard to see if he was hiding there, and pulled all the towels out of the closet when she thought she heard a duck snore from the back. From her high bedroom window, she kept a lookout, watching and waiting for her friend.

When autumn came, the brown ducks waggled out of the pond, wiggled dry and flew away in a tangle of brown wings. Bianca remembered the last time she'd seen Puddleduck, near the brown pair at the pond. She stared hard at the flock, searching for a flick of lavender or a winking eye. Just for a moment, one small fellow swerved from the others and seemed to notice Bianca, but then he, too, was gone.

The leaves stacked up like pages of a book outside Bianca's window, each one telling stories about caterpillars grown fat in the summer sun or twiggy nests hidden in their shade. She listened to these rustling murmurs as the leaves fell, but when she opened her window and asked about Puddleduck, the whispering stopped.

Her sister brought Bianca her stuffed dog with the autographed ears to keep until Puddleduck came home. Bianca smiled at her sister, but put the dog on the floor when her sister was gone.

Her father took her to a toy store and told her to pick any animal at all. There was a cuddly whiskered cat, and a cranky troll with shaggy hair. But there was no one like Puddleduck, a quacky, crabby duck with a soft spot for a little girl named Bianca. All these animals would be happy with other children, so Bianca left them to wait.

That winter, when Bianca sat in her father's lap to hear her nighttime stories, sometimes she forget to listen. If she stared straight ahead at the window, black with night, she saw a man and a girl in a rocker, the man reading and rocking, the girl staring back at her. There seemed to be an empty spot in the window, just under the girl's arm. Bianca would look away quickly, and squeeze closer to her father.

When the snow came, Bianca remembered how Puddleduck liked to sit on the window sill, watching her make snow ducks. So she made one, then came in to look at it from the window. It was just an ordinary duck, not a Puddleduck at all.

Finally, it was spring. Pink blossoms fluttered from the cherry tree, and the windy rain plastered them against Bianca's window. From where she watched, she could see the cool pond glisten impatiently, longing for the ducks' return.

At last the two brown ducks skimmed down onto the water, but with them this time was a third. This one was a muddied white duck with sharp eyes. He seemed to Bianca to have a lavender shine to his feathers.

Over the spring, Bianca watched him. When she wandered by the pond, the brown pair quacked their anger at her. But the other duck swam calmly past, sneaking quick glances from his inky eyes.
She knew it was Puddleduck, but no one else did.

She tried to tell her father, but when he came to the pond, all three ducks flew away in alarm. Her sister wouldn't even come to see. So Bianca sat by the edge alone, far enough away to calm the brown ducks, close enough to talk quietly to the white one, and sing him little songs.

One summer day she left him a drawing of herself and Puddleduck, tucked under the quilt asleep. The next morning it was gone.

Early in the autumn she crept close to the pond. Ignoring the brown ducks, she held out her hands to the little white duck. He watched her sharply and swam close by, just out of her reach. He was a wild duck now, not quite her Puddleduck.

One cool morning, Bianca woke to find all three ducks gone. She ran down to the pond without a sweater, her father calling after her. She searched until she found one white feather in the tall grasses. Slowly, she climbed the hill home, rubbing the feather between her palms, warmed by its lavender shine.

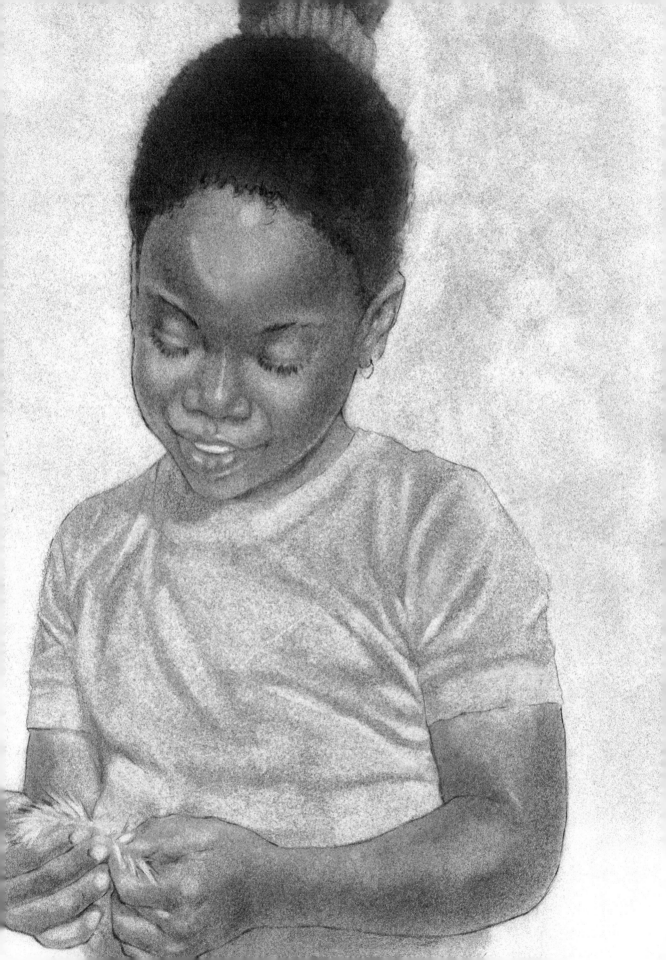

The next spring, Bianca was too busy with her schoolwork and lessons and new friends to think of checking the pond. She had given back her sister's autographed dog long ago. The noisy neighborhood swimming pool seemed much more fun than the quiet duck pond. And the year after that, Bianca and her family moved away, and she never saw the pond again.

Bianca grew up and had her own little girl. And one day she saw a little stuffed duck in a toy store. It reminded her so much of Puddleduck that she bought it and took it home to her daughter. That night, with her daughter and the duck cuddled against her, she told the story of a girl named Bianca and her friend, Puddleduck. When the story was over, her daughter was still for a moment and then said, "Mommy, won't you tell it again?" So she did.

*"That one spring, Bianca knew that Puddleduck would come back..."*